THE UNDERDOG GANG
AND THE CLASS PET

BY JOBY NELSON

Joby Nelson

FOR MY PARENTS

CHAPTERS

INTRODUCTION:

THE UNDERDOG GANG

This is an adventure story about The Underdog Gang, a group of five boys who love doing underdogs on the swings. They became best friends and saved recess for their school when their swings went missing.

First, there is David Stephenson. He has brown hair and a buzz cut. David is really into martial arts and practices every day.

Next, is Gavin Garrillis. He has blonde hair and wears striped shirts. Gavin loves playing games, especially video games.

Third, is Nick Thranter. He has blonde hair and always wears sports shirts. Nick is really into sports and knows about every professional athlete.

Next, is Rally Wills. He has black hair and wears glasses. Rally loves pulling pranks on his friends and always has a joke to tell.

Last, is Sim Igurt. He has brown hair and always wears a hat. Sim loves to read and solving things like Rubik's cubes and riddles.

DAVID   GAVIN   NICK   RALLY   SIM

CHAPTER 1:

THE CLASS PET

It was a pretty normal day at Gator Elementary School. Miss Gardner was teaching her students.

Among her students were David, Gavin, Nick, Rally and Sim.

"Now class," began Miss Gardner, "in two weeks we have the opportunity to go on a very special field trip to the zoo. The reason this field trip will be very special is we aren't going to walk around and see all of the exhibits. Instead, we are going to be zookeepers for the day and help take care of the animals."

The students shouted with excitement. They had never gone on a field trip like this before.

Miss Gardner continued, "Before we can go on the field trip, we have to learn about what it means to be responsible and how to work together. I am going to assign everyone to a group. Each group must work together to complete their assignment in order to be able to go on the field trip."

"The assignment is to take care of our new class pet by feeding him, giving him water and cleaning out his cage."

Miss Gardner stepped toward a table at the front of the classroom.

She pulled off a cloth to reveal a glass tank underneath.

Inside was a yellow and white snake.

"This is Slither," said Miss Gardner, "and this is his home. It is called a terrarium. It is a safe place for Slither to sleep, eat, play, and live."

"Each group will need to feed Slither and make sure he has plenty of water in his bowl every morning. There is a can on my desk labeled 'Snake Food.' Slither gets one scoop," explained Miss Gardner. "It is also very important to make sure to shut the lid on the terrarium when you are done."

"After each group cares for Slither, then they may come out and join the rest of the class at morning recess," continued Miss Gardner.

"If you want to go on the field trip, you will have to pass this assignment, and report back to the class about what you learned," explained Miss Gardner.

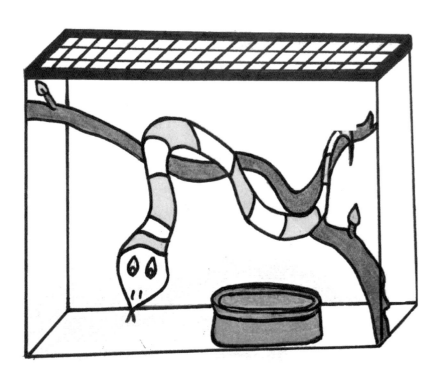

5

"Now," said Miss Gardner, "the first group to take care of Slither will be David, Gavin, Nick, Rally and Sim."

The boys looked up and blankly stared back at Miss Gardner.

While she had been giving instructions, they hadn't been paying attention.

They were too busy solving Rubik's cubes, having a staring contest and napping.

David was the only one who was paying attention.

The rest of the boys had no idea what Miss Gardner was talking about or what they were supposed to do.

CHAPTER 2:

THE LOST SNAKE

"What did Miss Gardner say we had to do?" asked Sim. "I wasn't paying attention. I was solving my new Rubik's cube."

"I don't know," said Rally, "but what is a snake's favorite subject in school?"

The boys stared at him.

"Hiss-tory," laughed Rally.

"This is no time for jokes," said David. "Our assignment is to take care of Slither. Miss Gardner said we can't go on the field trip to the zoo if we don't."

"Oh right. There's no way I'm missing out on a chance to feed a monkey," said Rally.

"But I want to go to recess now," whined Nick. "I have to work on my basketball skills for the free throw contest."

"Let's feed Slither his food, then we can go to recess," said David. "Miss Gardner said the snake food is on her desk."

The boys walked to Miss Gardner's desk and found the jar labeled, 'Snake Food'.

9

"I can give Slither the food," said Sim. "Rally, help me open the tank."

Rally took the lid off of the tank and set it on the table.

Sim put a big scoop of snake food into Slither's bowl.

"Look!" shouted Nick as he ran to the window. "The kids are playing basketball without me. I'll see you fellas outside."

He ran out of the classroom to recess.

"Hey, wait for us," shouted Gavin and Rally as they followed Nick outside.

"I fed Slither his food," Sim said to David, "Now let's go do some underdogs, yahoo!"

It was a really nice day to be outside.

The boys were having a great time swinging and playing basketball.

Suddenly, Sim stopped mid-underdog.

The swing hit him on the back of the head.

"Ouch," he screamed as he rubbed the back of his head.

"What is the matter with you?" asked David.

"I have to go find Rally," said Sim.

13

Sim ran to Rally who was in the middle of tying two girls' shoelaces together.

"Rally," said Sim, "did you put the lid back on Slither's tank after I fed him?"

"What?" asked Rally.

He looked upset that Sim had interrupted him from pulling a prank.

"Um, yeah, I totally did. Why?" asked Rally.

"Are you 100% sure you did, Rally?" Sim asked again.

Rally stopped tying the shoelaces together and stood up.

"Well, no Sim, I'm not 1-0-0 % sure that I did," said Rally. "What's the big deal?"

15

Sim's eyes got really big.

He grabbed Rally's arm and started running.

"Hurry up!" shouted Sim. "We have to get the rest of the gang."

Sim and Rally got The Underdog Gang from recess and they all ran back to their classroom.

"Why did we have to stop playing?" complained Nick out of breath from running.

"Yeah," whined Gavin, "recess was just getting fun. What's the problem?"

"That is the problem," said Sim.

He pointed to Slither's tank.

The boys looked at the tank, but didn't see anything.

"Rally never put the lid back on the tank after I fed Slither," Sim explained.

His voice was very serious and he had a scared look in his eyes.

"Now Slither is GONE!"

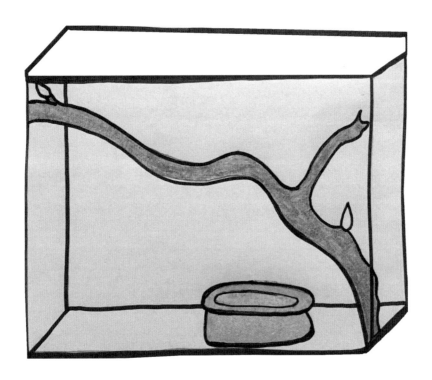

CHAPTER 3:

THE FAKE SNAKE

The boys stood together in silence looking at Slither's tank.

"What are we going to do?" David asked. "This is not good."

"Yeah, Miss Gardner said we can't go on the field trip if we don't do a good job taking care of Slither. Now we won't be able to go because we can't even find him. This is all your fault Rally," said Nick.

"My fault?" repeated Rally. "If you weren't so obsessed with playing basketball and shouting that the kids were playing outside without you, I wouldn't have gotten distracted and ran out to recess!"

"It doesn't matter whose fault it is," said Sim. "We need to find Slither and put him back in his tank before Miss Gardner and the class get back here. Recess is almost over so they will be here any minute."

The boys started looking all over the classroom for Slither.

They looked in the desks, under the trash can, behind the bookshelf, in the center materials, at the computer table, on the story time rug, in the art supplies, and under the chairs.

Slither was nowhere to be found.

"He must have left the classroom," said David. "Now we are really going to be in big trouble."

"I have an idea," said Sim. "What if we make a fake snake to put in the tank just until we can find where Slither is hiding? I bet Miss Gardner and the other kids won't even notice."

"That's a great idea," said David. "Hurry. We need to find something that will look like a snake."

The boys went around the room and each came back with a supply to make the fake snake.

They used David's yellow karate belt to make the body, buttons from Gavin's game controller for the eyes, white athletic tape from Nick for the stripes, a red pipe cleaner from Rally's prankster's kit for the tongue and Sim's creative solving knowledge to put it together.

"The fake Slither doesn't look too bad," said Gavin. The boys nodded, but were interrupted by voices coming down the hall.

"Agh, we have to hurry," said Sim.

The boys placed the fake Slither in his terrarium then went back to their seats.

As the classroom door opened and the class came in from recess, the boys nervously waited to see if anyone would notice the new fake Slither.

Luckily no one did.

The boys anxiously watched the clock until it was time to go home.

Finally, Miss Gardner announced, "Okay class, time to go home. Please pick up your things and line up."

As the boys got in line to go home, Sim said to The Underdog Gang, "Emergency meeting at my house today after school. We have to make a plan to find Slither."

The boys each gave him a thumbs up and headed to their pick up lines.

CHAPTER 4:

THE SNAKE PLAN

At Sim's house, The Underdog Gang got to work making a plan to find Slither.

"First, we need to research where snakes like to hide," said Sim. "Gavin, can you please use the computer to find out?"

Gavin smiled. He loved computers because they were just like video games. "I'll find all the information we need, fellas, don't worry," said Gavin.

He went to the computer to look up places snakes like to hide.

"Next, we need to make a map of the school and where we will search tomorrow. David can you help me create the map?" asked Sim.

David nodded.

"Finally, we have to figure out what problems we might have during the search and how we can avoid them. Rally and Nick are you up for this challenge?" Sim asked.

Both boys smiled.

Thirty minutes later the boys came back together to share what they had been working on.

First up was Gavin. "I found out snakes are very good at hiding and can squeeze into really small spaces. They can hide behind or under large appliances, on window ledges and door frames, near water pipes, close to heaters, and in ceiling rafters."

Next up was Sim and David. "We created a map of the school. Based on Gavin's research we think we should search these areas: the lockers in the hallway outside of our classroom, the ceiling in the gym, the music room down the hall and the boiler room where the furnace is."

"We put an "X" to each location on the map," explained Sim.

"Now, Rally and Nick, what obstacles or problems do you think we might have during our search?" asked David.

25

"Well, we think there might be four things that could be problems," said Nick.

"One, the ceilings in the gym are really high so we may not be able to see what is hiding on the rafters."

"Two, the music room is full of instruments so we need to make sure we don't knock any over and make noise."

"Three, we have to watch out for The Business Girls. They make a lot of hall monitor patrols and will tell on us if they find out what we are up to."

"Four, the boiler room is the most terrifying place we have ever heard about. It has large mechanical devices that make ear piercing sounds and frighten us to our core. We are afraid to imagine what doom awaits us if we go there. Plus it supposedly smells terrible."

"This is really good fellas," said Sim. "Let's plan to sneak out of recess tomorrow to look for Slither. With our master plan, we should be able to find Slither in no time."

The Underdog Gang all agreed. Operation "Find Slither" was a go.

CHAPTER 5:

OPERATION "FIND SLITHER"

The next day at school the boys stood at the back of the line to go out to recess.

Instead of going out to play, they ditched their class and formed a huddle in the bathroom.

"Okay," whispered Sim, "the first patrol by The Business Girls just went by. Now is the perfect time to search the lockers. Make sure to be as quiet as you can so we don't scare Slither or get in trouble."

"Ready, gang?"

"Let's go!"

The boys tiptoed down the hallway and started opening up lockers one by one.

Things were going smoothly.

The boys felt like they would find Slither in no time.

Suddenly, Gavin erupted with a high pitched, "Agggghhhh!"

It sounded like a combination of a tea kettle and a train whistle. The locker Gavin opened had hundreds of balls inside. The balls poured out on top of him and rolled all over the hallway!

At the same time, Nick shouted, "Oh my gosh!" A half-empty milk carton had spilled all over the front of him when he opened a locker.

"Great, now I smell like a baby who spit up milk. My vintage Michael Jordan jersey is ruined!" he cried.

Next they heard, "Gross. How disgusting! I just touched a moldy sandwich! Green goop is all over my hand and now I smell like a dirty diaper!" whined David.

Rally started laughing.

"It's not funny," said David.

"Sorry," said Rally, "look it's dripping all over your shoes."

Rally laughed so hard he lost his balance and tripped over the balls that were on the floor and he fell on top of Sim who was looking inside a locker.

"Guys, all of this noise is going to get us caught!" said Sim. "We'll never find Slither and we won't get to go on the field trip."

"But if we don't go on the field trip I'll never be able to live out my dreams of feeding cotton candy to an orangutan or riding on the back of a giraffe," said Rally.

"Rally, I don't think that's part of the field trip," replied Sim.

"Don't worry about it, we just need to be quiet or we'll get caught," said David sternly.

Just then, the boys heard the sound of footsteps coming down the hall.

"Hurry, into the gym," said Nick.

The boys ran into the gym and shut the door behind them, just before the footsteps came around the corner.

"That was close," said Gavin. "While we are in here, should we see if Slither is hiding on the ceiling rafters?"

The boys strained their necks upward to see if Slither was hiding on the rafters.

They started leaning so far back to look up that they each lost their balance and fell backward.

33

"It's no use," said Gavin. "The ceiling is too high for us to see up on the rafters and there isn't a ladder. Slither isn't up there."

"Ok, what's next on the map?" asked David.

"The music room," said Sim. "Let's go."

The boys went next door to the music room.

Rally and Nick were correct. The room was littered with every kind of musical instrument imaginable. There were tambourines on the floor, trumpets on chairs, triangles on shelves, and even two glockenspiels on a desk. Every part of the room was full of instruments and music stands.

"Okay, let's search the room and every instrument," said Sim. "Slither might be hiding inside. But remember, be quiet."

The boys started looking. They turned over the instruments hoping Slither would appear, but he didn't. Then they heard a loud clanging sound.

"What in the world!" shouted Gavin.

Standing behind a large metal gong was Rally.

"Rally! What are you doing?" said David. "The whole school probably heard you! You are going to scare Slither away! Put that down."

"Oh, sorry guys," said Rally. "It's the biggest gong I've ever seen. I had to play it. I'll make it up to you. Where's the next place we planned to search?"

The boys looked at their map.

Every room had been crossed off of the list except one place the boys were afraid to go...the boiler room.

"We can do this, fellas," said David. "I'm trained in martial arts and nothing scares me. I will lead the way."

"Oh man," said Nick, "just thinking of that place makes my stomach feel like the time my grandpa accidentally gave me spoiled milk."

"Come on guys, if we don't find Slither we'll never get to go to the zoo to swim with dolphins and train wolves to be our protectors," said Rally.

"Umm, Rally, have you ever been to a zoo before?" asked Sim. "None of those things happen there."

"Never mind," said Gavin. "It's time to find Slither."

The boys started walking slowly towards the boiler room which was the last room at the end of the hallway.

David opened the door with a kick and motioned to the boys that the room was safe to enter.

Gavin and Sim went inside first.

Nick and Rally were about to go in when they heard the unmistakable sound of a hall monitor whistle.

Then they heard a voice say, "What do you think you are doing?"

The boys turned around.

Standing in front of them were three girls.

They each had bright yellow reflector vests.

These three girls were who Rally and Nick had warned the gang about.

They were their worst nightmare.

They were The Business Girls.

A group of girls Principal Snapper had appointed to patrol the hallways of Gator Elementary School.

If you were caught, the punishment was severe...detention for an entire week.

39

"Um, we were just looking for you," explained Rally.

"Yeah," lied Nick. "Rally thinks that girls can't throw a football, but I told him he was wrong. We came to find you because I know you girls can throw a football farther than Rally can."

The girls looked at each other and laughed. "Oh, Rally you're wrong," said the tallest Business Girl. "We challenge you to a game of football right here, right now. Us versus you. If you win, we will let you go. But if you lose, we're telling Principal Snapper on you."

Nick and Rally looked at each other.

They really didn't want to play football, but they also really didn't want to go to the boiler room.

So they decided to distract The Business Girls so David, Gavin and Sim could search the boiler room for Slither.

"You have a deal," replied Nick, as he shook the girls' hands.

CHAPTER 6:

A GIANT RAT

Nick and Rally played the best game of football they had ever played.

The Business Girls were tough competition, but the boys won 21-20 on a missed extra point.

"Wow, great job Rally!" said Nick.

"Thanks. You did a great job, too," said Rally.

They started to sit down at the end of the hallway, when the boiler room door opened hitting Nick.

"Ouch," he screamed rubbing his elbow.

"Sorry," said Gavin. "I didn't see you there."

"So was Slither inside?" asked Rally.

"Nope and we looked everywhere," said David.

Gavin, David and Sim joined Nick and Rally and sat down on the floor.

"Man, I really thought we would find Slither with Operation 'Find Slither'," said Sim. "What are we going to do? Miss Gardner will be so disappointed that we lost Slither."

"If we don't go on the field trip, how will I ever learn how to shear the wool from sheep and make it into clothing?" asked Rally.

"Yeah, what a bummer Rally," said Nick as he rolled his eyes. He leaned his head back really hard on the wall. All of a sudden Nick fell backward.

A burst of light blinded the boys.

Past Nick the boys could see a door which opened up to a secret room.

The boys were shocked.

They stood up and walked inside.

"What is this place?" asked Gavin.

The room had many unfamiliar objects inside.

Things the boys had never seen before.

Tall tables with goggles, shelves with glass objects, devices hanging from the ceiling, and jars full of strange looking balls.

The boys also saw plants, books, metal cages and glass tanks.

The room was pretty big and smelled like an old, wet gym sock.

"This must be the 5th graders' secret science lab," stated Sim. "I always thought it was a myth, but it's a real place."

The boys turned and saw a huge terrarium, much bigger than the one in their class.

"Do you think Slither could have slithered his way in there?" asked Nick.

"According to my research that would be the exact place a snake would hide," said Gavin. "There's only one way to find out."

Gavin cautiously opened the door to the terrarium.

They heard a loud rustling sound. The plants inside the terrarium began to shake. Something was moving toward them.

"That sounds too big for a snake," said Sim. "What could it..."

But before Sim could finish his sentence, a furry creature the boys had never seen before burst out of the terrarium and headed straight for them!

"What is that thing!?" screamed David.

"It's some kind of enormous squirrel or a super athletic gopher!" shouted Gavin.

"No it's some kind of half rabbit, half dog!" cried Sim.

It's going to eat us!" screamed Nick.

"I don't care what it is, we have to get out of here," shouted Sim. "RUN!!!"

The boys ran to the other side of the classroom, but the squirrel/gopher/rabbit/dog chased after them.

The boys screamed, "Yaaaaaahhhhhh!!!"

They ran all around the classroom, bumping into things and knocking stuff over.

Things started breaking.

The boys terrified of the creature, bumped and crashed into each other.

The boys scrambled to get up, but just as they did, they saw something fly over their heads, and land on top of the creature.

It was a giant net.

The creature was trapped.

CHAPTER 7:

A SURPRISE HELPER

The boys were relieved. They looked behind them to see what had saved them and were stunned at who they saw.

"Mr. Wizardman!" Gavin said.

The boys looked up and saw their old friend Mr. Wizardman waving at them.

They had met Mr. Wizardman during another Underdog Gang adventure. The boys thought he had stolen their swings when they went missing on the playground, (but really Mr. Wizardman was just fixing them).

"Hey boys!" said Mr. Wizardman. "It's great to see you! Why are you chasing my capybara?"

The boys looked confused.

"What are you doing here Mr. Wizardman?" asked Gavin.

"Yeah, and what is a capybara?" asked Sim.

"Well boys, you know how much I love making sure kids have fun at recess. I also love animals. My Wizard Playground Repair business is going so well, I decided to open a pet store. I was talking to Principal Snapper the other day and we thought it would be a good idea if the students at Gator Elementary School learned about animals and how to take care of them. I brought some of the pets from my store to the school so each class could take care of one to learn responsibility," explained Mr. Wizardman.

"This little fella right here, is my capybara. His name is Lemmy. The older students are taking care of him in the science lab. Capybaras are the largest rodents in the world. They are native to South America. You might have seen their cousins before – guinea pigs?" said Mr. Wizardman.

Mr. Wizardman took the net off of Lemmy, picked him up and gave him a hug.

The boys slowly nodded with puzzled looks on their faces.

"Why was Lemmy chasing us all over the place? We could've been hurt," said Sim.

"Nah, Lemmy is really friendly. He loves going on walks and snuggling. He also loves to eat grass and plants. He probably thought you were here to feed him and that is probably why he was chasing you," explained Mr. Wizardman.

"Do any of you have food in your pockets?" asked Mr. Wizardman.

Rally looked surprised. How did Mr. Wizardman know that he thought.

"I do," said Rally. He pulled out a piece of cheese.

"Agh," said Nick. "Who cut the cheese?" He moved his hands in front of his face to fan away the odor.

The rest of the boys plugged their noses.

"Why do you have cheese in your pocket, Rally?" asked Sim.

"Well, sometimes I get hungry and want a snack," said Rally.

"You could pick something better than stinky cheese to keep in your pocket," said David.

The other boys nodded.

55

"It's okay, Rally," said Mr. Wizardman. "No one was hurt. It's time for Lemmy to eat. Would you boys like to help me put Lemmy back in his home and feed him?"

The boys agreed and followed Mr. Wizardman to Lemmy's cage.

"That's his food over there on the desk," pointed Mr. Wizardman. "He gets one big scoop in his bowl."

Rally went and got the food. He brought it to Lemmy's bowl.

"Say," said Mr. Wizardman, "what are you boys doing in the science lab anyway?"

The boys gathered around Mr. Wizardman and they explained the whole story.

How they were supposed to take care of Slither, but they lost him.

How they made a plan to find Slither, but couldn't.

How they would never be able to go on their class field trip because they lost Slither.

And how they accidently found the science lab, but were chased by a capybara.

57

"Well boys, it's a good thing you ran into me," said Mr. Wizardman. "Slither and I are best buds. I know all about snakes. I also have a pretty good idea where Slither is probably hiding."

CHAPTER 8:

MISSION ACCOMPLISHED

The boys followed Mr. Wizardman out of the science lab and back down the long hallway to their classroom.

He started to open the door.

"Mr. Wizardman, what are we doing back at our classroom?" asked Nick. "We've already looked everywhere in here for Slither and we couldn't find him."

"No worries, Nick," said Mr. Wizardman. "Like I said before, I have a pretty good guess where Slither is hiding. When we play hide and seek at my store, I always find him in the same hiding spot."

Mr. Wizardman walked all the way to the back of the classroom.

He knelt down and started picking paper out of a metal trash can.

Then, Mr. Wizardman slowly tipped the trash can on its' side so the boys could peer inside.

"Come closer," invited Mr. Wizardman with a smile.

At the bottom of the trash can, coiled into a circle, was Slither.

The boys couldn't believe it. Slither had been in their classroom the entire time!

"Slither!" the boys shouted in unison.

"Thank you so much, Mr. Wizardman!" said David.

"Yeah, you are just the best," shouted Nick. He gave Mr. Wizardman a big hug.

"No problem at all boys," said Mr. Wizardman.

"This is great," said Sim, "but we have to hurry and put Slither in his tank before the class comes back from recess."

Rally picked Slither up and The Underdog Gang hurried to Slither's tank.

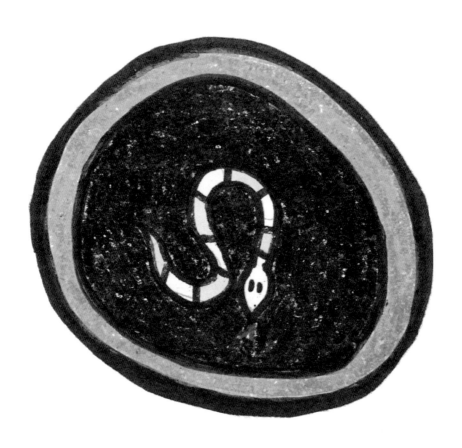

61

The boys were startled to hear someone behind them clearing their throat.

They turned around to see Miss Gardner looking at them.

"What's going on here, boys?" asked Miss Gardner.

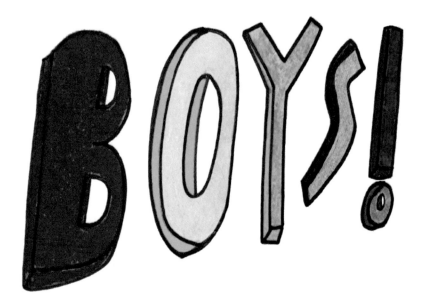

The Underdog Gang didn't know what to say.

They were afraid they had been caught.

Did Miss Gardner know that Slither had been lost?

Had she found their fake snake?

Did she see them trying to put Slither back in his tank before the class came in from recess?

Was she on to them?

All of these questions crossed their minds.

Before they could think of a response Miss Gardner said, "Oh, it looks like you were just cleaning up Slither's terrarium. I hope you all had fun taking care of him. Now it's time for your presentation about caring for Slither. Are you ready?"

Remembering back to all the research he had done on snakes Gavin said, "We sure are Miss Gardner."

"Yeah, we learned a lot of important things about snakes and how to care for them. We also learned about another animal. Can we earn extra credit if we share that information with the class as well?" Sim asked.

"That would be wonderful boys," replied Miss Gardner.

The Underdog Gang gave their presentation and taught the class all about snakes and capybaras.

Most of the kids had never even heard of a capybara.

Miss Gardner asked the boys how they learned so much so quickly.

"Well, we did get a little help from an old friend," said Sim.

He looked to the back of the classroom where Mr. Wizardman was standing.

Mr. Wizardman quietly gave the boys an approving two thumbs up, but when the rest of the class turned to see what Sim was looking at, *POOF*, the Wizardman had disappeared.

The class clapped when the boys were done.

"Well, boys, that was very impressive," said Miss Gardner. "I can tell you learned a lot about snakes and capybaras. But most importantly you learned about responsibility and working together."

"Yes, we learned when we work together we can accomplish much more than when we work alone," said Sim.

"We are all good at different things and that is what makes us a great team. We stuck together making plans and supported each other," said David.

"We overcame every obstacle that was thrown at us and we learned a lot about responsibility," said Gavin.

"We even had some laughs and helped each other face some of our deepest fears," explained Nick.

"And that's why we are THE UNDERDOG GANG!" shouted Rally.

"Well, I am happy to report that each of you will be able to go on the field trip to the zoo," said Ms. Gardner. "I am also giving each of you five extra minutes at recess tomorrow for teaching the class about capybaras."

The boys high-fived each other.

Extra time at recess meant more time for doing underdogs.

As the boys lined up to go home that day Nick said to The Underdog Gang, "Hey fellas that was another fun adventure we had together. We should write another story about it."

"That's a great idea Nick," said Sim. "Come over to my house after school and we can work on our second book together."

The boys nodded and gave a thumbs up.

"But first...Rally, take that stinky cheese out of your pocket."

The boys all laughed.

THE END.

THE SECOND AWESOME BOOK:

THE UNDERDOG GANG AND THE CLASS PET

They were supposed to take care of their class pet...
But Lost Him!

A HUGE RAT CHASED
THEM EVERYWHERE!

HUGERAT!
↓

72

But then a friend came and helped them find Slither.

Everything was good again, and they could go on a field trip.

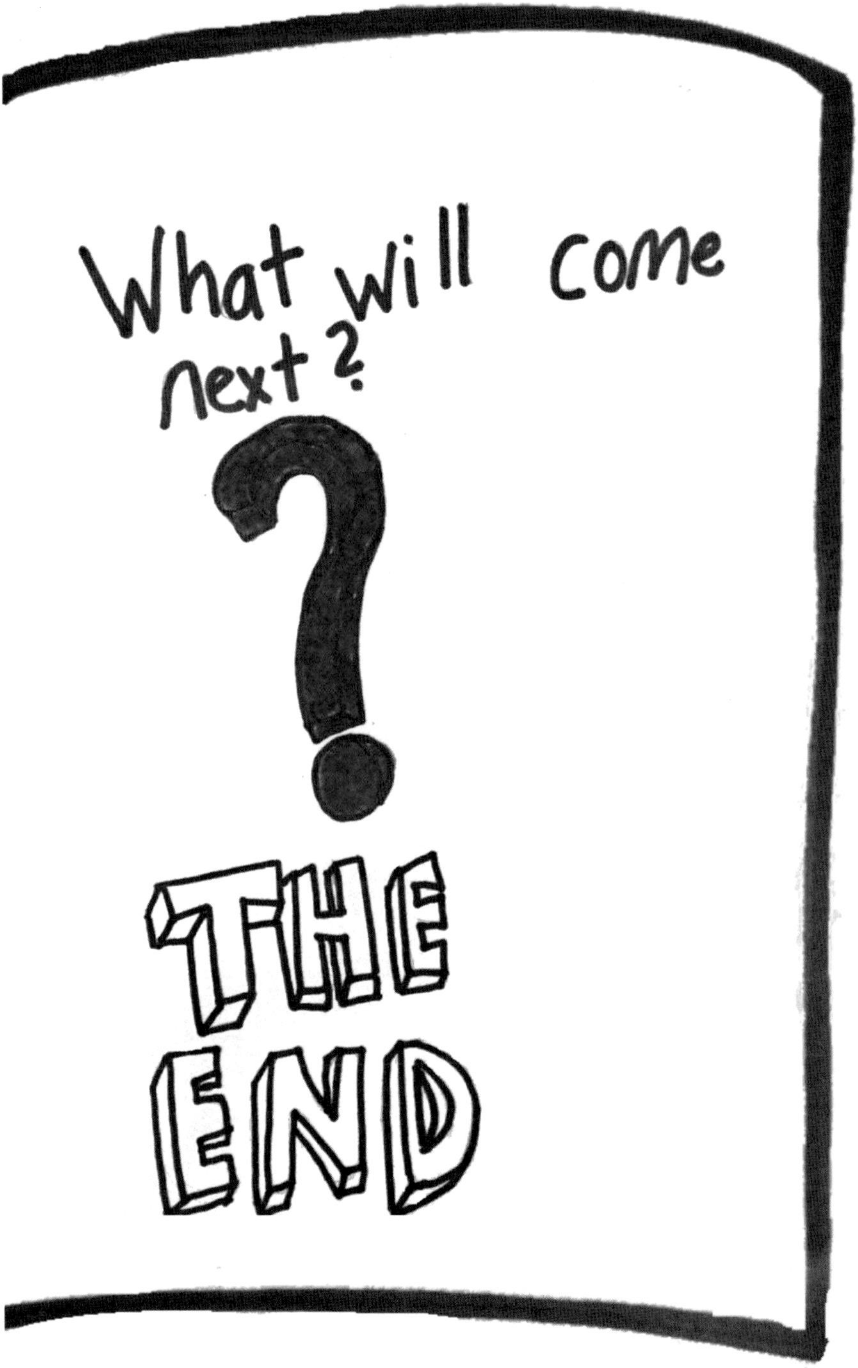
What will come next?
THE END

ABOUT THE AUTHOR

JOBY NELSON HAS LOVED TO READ AND DRAW PICTURES SINCE HE WAS FIVE YEARS OLD. WHEN JOBY WAS IN KINDERGARTEN HE WOULD SIT AT HIS KITCHEN TABLE AND MAKE BOOKS USING NOTEBOOK PAPER AND #2 PENCILS. IN FIRST GRADE, HE WANTED TO BECOME A "REAL" AUTHOR AND PUBLISHED HIS FIRST "REAL" ADVENTURE BOOK SO KIDS IN HIS CLASS WOULD LAUGH AND LOVE TO READ AS MUCH AS HE DOES.

READ MORE SILLY ADVENTURES ABOUT THE UNDERDOG GANG IN:

FOLLOW ALONG ON FACEBOOK: @AUTHORJOBYNELSON

Made in the USA
Lexington, KY
15 November 2019